This book belongs to

_____

_____

To my husband, Jan,
who showed me Vienna and so much more…
—L.R.L.

For Peter and Jacqui Poole and all your grandchildren
—Love from Alison

THIS IS A BORZOI BOOK PUBLISHED BY ALFRED A. KNOPF

Text copyright © 2014 by Linda Ravin Lodding
Jacket art and interior illustrations copyright © 2014 by Alison Jay

All rights reserved. Published in the United States by Alfred A. Knopf, an imprint of
Random House Children's Books, a division of Random House, Inc., New York.
Originally published in slightly different form in Great Britain by Gullane Children's Books, London, in 2014.

Knopf, Borzoi Books, and the colophon are registered trademarks of Random House, Inc.

Visit us on the Web! randomhouse.com/kids

Educators and librarians, for a variety of teaching tools, visit us at RHTeachersLibrarians.com

Library of Congress Cataloging-in-Publication Data is available upon request.
ISBN 978-0-385-75331-9 (trade)
ISBN 978-0-385-75332-6 (lib. bdg.)

The illustrations in this book were created using alkyd paint and crackle varnish on thick cartridge paper.

MANUFACTURED IN CHINA
March 2014
10 9 8 7 6 5 4 3 2 1
First American Edition

A Gift for Mama

by Linda Ravin Lodding • illustrated by Alison Jay

ALFRED A. KNOPF NEW YORK

Morning bells rang out over Vienna.
Shoppers and sellers filled the streets, and
carriages clippity-clopped against the cobblestones.
Oskar peered wide-eyed into the shop windows.

It was his mother's birthday, and he wanted
to give her the perfect gift.

The windows were full of treasures.
Cakes, hats, music boxes . . .
What can I buy?
wondered Oskar.

He had only
a single coin.

But there, in the middle of the
market, was a flower seller.
A beautiful yellow rose peeked out
from within her basket of blooms.

GRABEN

Schloss

Augarten

The perfect present, thought Oskar, and held out his coin.

As Oskar admired his gift, an artist passed by.
"What a wonderful rose!" he exclaimed.
"How perfect it would be
in the portrait I'm painting!"

"But it's a present for my mama,"
explained Oskar.

"I'll trade you," said the artist. "What do you say—
a beautiful horsehair paintbrush for that beautiful rose?"

Oskar hesitated. . . .

But then he said,

"Of course!
I can paint a picture for Mama—
the perfect present!"

Oskar skipped toward home.

As he passed the Opera House,
he could hear the orchestra rehearsing.
He waved his paintbrush in time with the music.

Just then, a man came running toward him.
"I can't find my conductor's baton!" he cried. "Oh, what will I do?"

Suddenly the conductor beamed with delight.
"*You* have a baton!" he exclaimed.
"Sir, you are mistaken," said Oskar.

"This is a paintbrush."

"Paintbrush, baton, no matter. It can lead an orchestra!"

The conductor held up
a sheet of music.
"I'll trade you!
Here's a melody
I wrote just this morning.

Da Da Da Dee Dum,"
he sang.
"*Da Da Da Dee Dum.*"

"Mama loves music!" said Oskar.
"That's the perfect present."

"Da Da Da Dee Dum,
Dee Dee, Dum Dum....,"
sang Oskar as he waltzed
down the street.

"Da Da Da Dee Dum,"
Dee Dee, Dum Dum...!
another voice joined in.

"That tune," said the man.
"I have the perfect words for it! May I?"
He plucked the music from
Oskar's hand and started to write.

"But that's Mama's birthday song!"
Oskar cried.

"Now I have no present!"

The man rummaged through his satchel.
"Does your mama like books?"
he asked.
"I wrote this one myself."

"Mama loves books,"
said Oskar.

"A book is the perfect present!"

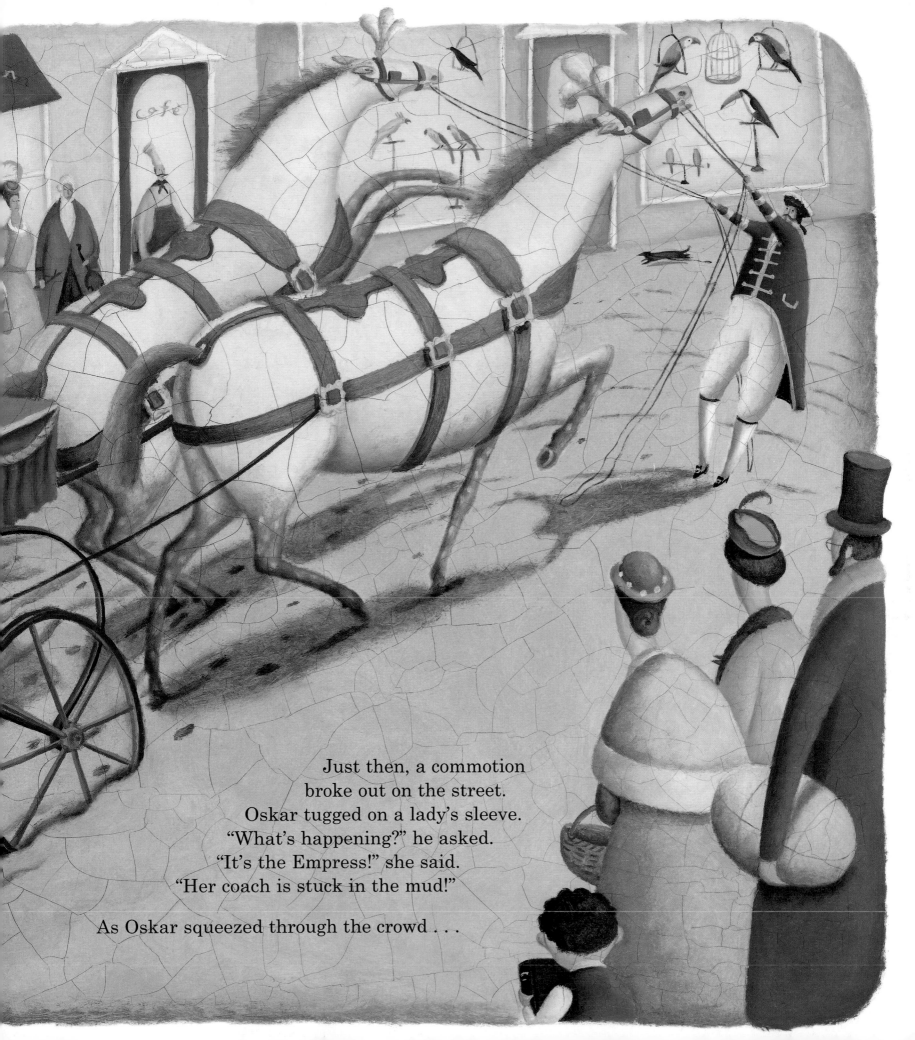

Just then, a commotion
broke out on the street.
Oskar tugged on a lady's sleeve.
"What's happening?" he asked.
"It's the Empress!" she said.
"Her coach is stuck in the mud!"

As Oskar squeezed through the crowd . . .

. . . suddenly a coachman grabbed his book!
He jammed it under the wheel. "Make way!" he shouted.

With a tug on the reins, the carriage lurched to a roll.
"Mama's book!" cried Oskar. "It's ruined."

But as Oskar looked up, there was the Empress herself!
She held out a box. "Candied violets," she said kindly. "To say sorry for your book."

Oskar bowed. "Thank you, Your Highness!"
The dainty, delicious sweets were the perfect gift for Mama!

Oskar ran along the banks of the river Danube.
He couldn't wait to see Mama's face. . . .

But there, on the water's edge,
a girl caught his eye. Even
though her face was covered in tears,
she was the prettiest girl he had ever seen.

"Why are you crying?" asked Oskar.
"Today is my mama's birthday," said the girl.
"An artist was painting my portrait for her.
But he couldn't finish it in time—"

"And now you have no present?" Oskar guessed.
The girl nodded and wiped away a tear.

Oskar held tightly to his box of sweets.

Then, ever so slowly, his fingers loosened.
"Here," he said gently, "give your mama these."

The girl's smile was as sweet as the scent
of the yellow rose pinned to her dress.
"The perfect present!" she said.

Oskar turned toward home.
Dusk was falling, and he knew
Mama would be worried.
He blinked back tears. . . .

What would he
give Mama now?

But suddenly there was
a tap on his shoulder.

"For you," said the girl.
And she handed him
the beautiful yellow rose.

Oskar's heart soared!
Clutching his gift,
he raced through the
darkening streets toward home.

Mama was waiting on the doorstep.
"Happy birthday!" cried Oskar.

Mama smelled the rose.
She wrapped her son in her arms.
"*Perfect,*" she said.

A Note from the Author

In 1994, when I moved to Vienna, I would walk the
cobblestone streets of the "old town" and imagine what this city must
have been like at the turn of the last century. It wasn't hard to picture:
Vienna in 1994 didn't look much different from Vienna in 1894. As I strolled
under the arches of the Hofburg Palace, passed the Opera House and
lingered in front of Demel's coffeehouse—eyeing their candied violets!—
a story came to me. I imagined a boy, Oskar, darting through the old town,
encountering the famous nineteenth-century artists, musicians,
writers and nobility. Everywhere I walked with Oskar, I could
see their shadows in this city—the artist Gustav Klimt,
the musician and composer Johann Strauss II,
the author Felix Salten and the beautiful Empress Sisi.
While *A Gift for Mama* is Oskar's story, this is also
Vienna's story. And now it's yours, too.

Linda Ravin Lodding